ON NEW YEAR'S DAY

TO THE DREAMERS, THE DOERS, AND THE

ONES WHO CELEBRATE LIFE'S LITTLE

MOMENTS—MAY EACH NEW YEAR BRING

ON NEW YEAR'S DAY

AS THE FIRST LIGHT OF MORNING TOUCHED THE SNOWY FOREST, OLIVER THE OWL PERCHED PROUDLY ON A BRANCH OVERLOOKING THE CLEARING WHERE THE NEW YEAR'S CELEBRATION WOULD SOON BEGIN. WEARING HIS SMALL TOP HAT AND WITH HIS CLOCK NECKLACE TICKING SOFTLY, HE CALLED OUT TO THE OTHER ANIMALS, "ONLY FOUR HOURS UNTIL NOON!" OLIVER HAD THE IMPORTANT JOB OF KEEPING TIME FOR THE BIG EVENT. HIS WISE EYES SPARKLED AS HE CAREFULLY COUNTED EACH HOUR, REMINDING EVERYONE TO FINISH THEIR PREPARATIONS. WHEN THE FINAL HOUR ARRIVED, OLIVER TOOK A DEEP BREATH, SPREAD HIS WINGS, AND LED THE COUNTDOWN WITH A CALM BUT EXCITED HOOT, GUIDING ALL HIS FRIENDS IN A JOYFUL CHEER TO WELCOME THE NEW YEAR.

OLIVER THE OWL

KINDNESS GOAL:

OWL'S KINDNESS GOAL IS TO TEACH HIS YOUNGER FRIENDS ABOUT THE STARS AND HOW TO FIND THEIR WAY BY MOONLIGHT, HELPING THEM FEEL SAFE AND CONFIDENT AT NIGHT.

RESOLUTION:

OWL'S RESOLUTION IS TO TRY NEW FOODS THIS YEAR, EXPLORING TREATS IN THE FOREST HE'S NEVER TASTED BEFORE.

DID YOU KNOW?

IN DIFFERENT PARTS OF THE WORLD, PEOPLE CELEBRATE NEW YEAR'S DAY WITH UNIQUE TRADITIONS! FOR EXAMPLE, IN SPAIN, IT'S COMMON TO EAT TWELVE GRAPES AT MIDNIGHT, ONE FOR EACH CHIME OF THE CLOCK, TO BRING GOOD LUCK. MANY ANIMALS, LIKE THE OWL, HAVE NATURAL WAYS OF MEASURING TIME. OWLS ARE NOCTURNAL AND USE THE QUIET NIGHTTIME HOURS FOR HUNTING, MAKING THEM EXCELLENT NATURAL TIMEKEEPERS!

ON NEW YEAR'S DAY

SOPHIE THE SQUIRREL ZIPPED THROUGH THE FOREST, HER SPARKLY "HAPPY NEW YEAR" SASH GLITTERING AS SHE DASHED FROM TREE TO TREE. SHE CLUTCHED A NOISEMAKER IN ONE PAW AND GATHERED PINECONES, BERRIES, AND ACORNS WITH THE OTHER, PREPARING DECORATIONS FOR THE BIG NEW YEAR'S CELEBRATION. SOPHIE'S JOB WAS TO MAKE EVERYTHING LOOK FESTIVE, AND SHE TOOK HER ROLE VERY SERIOUSLY. SHE ARRANGED PINECONES IN PATTERNS AND HUNG BERRIES ON BRANCHES LIKE ORNAMENTS. WHEN IT WAS FINALLY TIME, SOPHIE DARTED TO THE CLEARING, SQUEAKING WITH EXCITEMENT AS SHE AND HER FRIENDS CHEERED TO WELCOME THE NEW YEAR!

SOPHIE THE SQUIRREL

KINDNESS GOAL:
SQUIRREL'S KINDNESS GOAL IS TO SHARE SOME OF HER GATHERED FOOD WITH FRIENDS WHO MIGHT NEED IT DURING THE COLDER MONTHS.

RESOLUTION:
SQUIRREL'S RESOLUTION IS TO SLOW DOWN AND ENJOY MORE QUIET MOMENTS IN NATURE.

DID YOU KNOW?

IN MANY CULTURES, PEOPLE DECORATE THEIR HOMES WITH FESTIVE ITEMS TO WELCOME THE NEW YEAR, BELIEVING IT BRINGS GOOD LUCK. SIMILARLY, SQUIRRELS HELP "DECORATE" THE FOREST YEAR-ROUND. AS THEY HIDE NUTS AND ACORNS, THEY OFTEN FORGET WHERE THEY BURIED THEM, WHICH HELPS NEW TREES GROW AND KEEPS THE FOREST THRIVING!

ON NEW YEAR'S DAY

BRODY THE BEAR LUMBERED THROUGH HIS DEN, ARRANGING A COZY SPACE FOR HIS FRIENDS TO GATHER. HE WORE HIS FAVORITE SCARF, THE ONE WITH LITTLE STARS, AND HAD A PARTY HORN HANGING AROUND HIS NECK FOR THE BIG MOMENT. BRODY LOVED BEING THE HOST; HIS DEN WAS WARM AND FILLED WITH SOFT PINE NEEDLES FOR SEATING. HE STACKED LOGS FOR ANIMALS TO PERCH ON AND SET UP A SPECIAL SPOT FOR EVERYONE TO PLACE THEIR SNACKS. AS THE ANIMALS ARRIVED, BRODY WELCOMED EACH ONE WITH A WARM SMILE, READY TO CELEBRATE THE NEW YEAR TOGETHER.

BRODY THE BEAR

RESOLUTION: *BEAR'S RESOLUTION IS TO KEEP HIS DEN TIDIER THIS YEAR SO HE'S ALWAYS READY FOR VISITORS.*

KINDNESS GOAL: *BEAR'S KINDNESS GOAL IS TO INVITE SMALLER ANIMALS TO WARM UP IN HIS DEN DURING EXTRA COLD DAYS.*

DID YOU KNOW?

NEW YEAR'S CELEBRATIONS AROUND THE WORLD OFTEN INVOLVE GATHERING WITH FAMILY AND FRIENDS TO SHARE FOOD AND WARMTH. BEARS, TOO, CREATE COZY SPACES FOR THEMSELVES IN WINTER. ALTHOUGH MOST BEARS HIBERNATE, THEY PREPARE THEIR DENS CAREFULLY, GATHERING LEAVES AND BRANCHES TO MAKE A WARM PLACE TO SLEEP UNTIL SPRING!

ON NEW YEAR'S DAY

FERGUS THE FOX PRANCED THROUGH THE SNOWY FOREST, HIS RED BOW TIE GLEAMING AS HE PROUDLY LED THE NEW YEAR'S PARADE. WITH A SHINY RIBBON TIED TO HIS TAIL, HE TWIRLED AND DASHED AROUND, ENCOURAGING THE OTHER ANIMALS TO FOLLOW ALONG. FERGUS KNEW ALL THE BEST PATHS THROUGH THE WOODS, AND WITH EACH STEP, HE MADE THE PARADE FEEL EXTRA SPECIAL. HE EVEN ADDED A FEW FANCY SPINS AND JUMPS TO KEEP EVERYONE SMILING AND LAUGHING. WHEN THEY REACHED THE CLEARING, FERGUS BOWED AND GAVE A CHEERFUL GRIN, KNOWING HE'D MADE THE CELEBRATION UNFORGETTABLE.

FERGUS THE FOX

KINDNESS GOAL:
FOX'S KINDNESS GOAL IS TO HELP GUIDE LOST ANIMALS THROUGH THE FOREST AND SHOW THEM SAFE PATHS HOME.

RESOLUTION:
FOX'S RESOLUTION IS TO EXPLORE NEW PARTS OF THE FOREST, HOPING TO FIND HIDDEN TREASURES AND NEW ADVENTURES..

DID YOU KNOW?

MANY PEOPLE CELEBRATE NEW YEAR'S DAY WITH PARADES, COMPLETE WITH MUSIC AND FESTIVE DECORATIONS. IN THE WILD, FOXES ARE KNOWN FOR THEIR PLAYFUL BEHAVIOR AND AGILITY. THEY OFTEN LEAP AND POUNCE WHILE HUNTING OR PLAYING, USING THEIR KEEN SENSES TO NAVIGATE THROUGH THE FOREST.

ON NEW YEAR'S DAY

PEARL THE PEACOCK STRUTTED TO THE CENTER OF THE SNOWY CLEARING, HER GLITTERING FEATHERS FANNED OUT IN A SPECTACULAR DISPLAY. SHE WORE A LITTLE TIARA PERCHED PROUDLY ON HER HEAD, AND EACH FEATHER SPARKLED IN THE WINTER SUNLIGHT. AS SHE SHOWED OFF HER COLORS, THE OTHER ANIMALS CLAPPED AND CHEERED, MARVELING AT THE BEAUTIFUL SIGHT. PEARL LOVED BRINGING JOY TO HER FRIENDS, AND HER DAZZLING FEATHERS MADE THE NEW YEAR'S CELEBRATION FEEL EVEN MORE MAGICAL. WITH EACH TURN AND FLICK OF HER TAIL, SHE CREATED A RAINBOW OF COLORS THAT MADE THE SNOWY FOREST GLOW.

PEARL THE PEACOCK

KINDNESS GOAL:
PEARL'S KINDNESS GOAL IS TO SPREAD CHEER BY VISITING OTHER ANIMALS, BRIGHTENING THEIR DAYS WITH HER COLORFUL FEATHERS.

RESOLUTION:
PEARL'S RESOLUTION IS TO PRACTICE KINDNESS BY SHARING HER BEAUTY WITH OTHERS INSTEAD OF JUST KEEPING IT TO HERSELF.

DID YOU KNOW?

IN MANY CULTURES, PEOPLE DRESS UP AND WEAR SPECIAL OUTFITS FOR NEW YEAR'S CELEBRATIONS TO BRING IN GOOD LUCK. PEACOCKS NATURALLY DISPLAY THEIR COLORFUL TAIL FEATHERS TO IMPRESS OTHERS, ESPECIALLY DURING COURTSHIP. THEIR BEAUTIFUL FEATHERS HELP THEM STAND OUT AND ARE ONE OF NATURE'S MOST IMPRESSIVE SHOWS!

ON NEW YEAR'S DAY

ROSIE THE RABBIT HOPPED THROUGH THE SNOWY MEADOW, HER PARTY HAT'S POM-POM BOUNCING WITH EACH JOYFUL LEAP. CLUTCHED IN HER PAWS WAS A BOUQUET OF FRESH CARROTS TIED WITH A BRIGHT RIBBON—HER SPECIAL CONTRIBUTION TO THE NEW YEAR'S FEAST. ROSIE LOVED SHARING HER FAVORITE TREATS WITH FRIENDS. AS SHE ARRIVED AT BEAR'S COZY DEN, THE WARM GLOW OF LANTERNS AND THE SCENT OF PINE WELCOMED HER. ROSIE ARRANGED THE CARROTS ON THE FEAST TABLE, ADDING A SPLASH OF COLOR. WITH A CHEERFUL SMILE, SHE JOINED HER FRIENDS, EXCITED TO COUNT DOWN TO NOON AND WELCOME THE NEW YEAR TOGETHER.

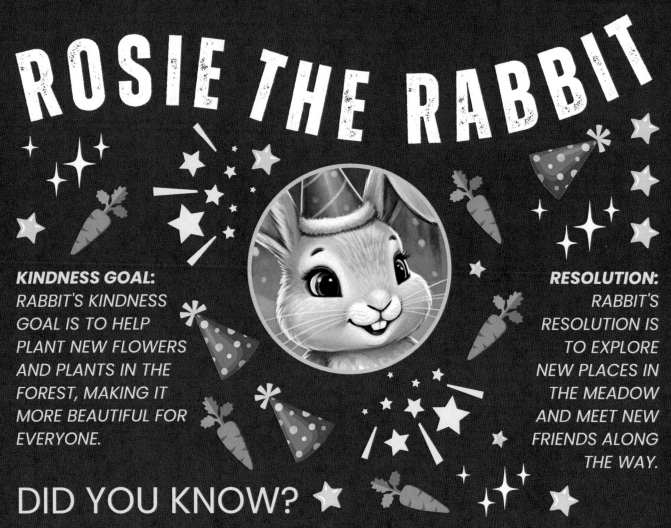

ROSIE THE RABBIT

KINDNESS GOAL:
RABBIT'S KINDNESS GOAL IS TO HELP PLANT NEW FLOWERS AND PLANTS IN THE FOREST, MAKING IT MORE BEAUTIFUL FOR EVERYONE.

RESOLUTION:
RABBIT'S RESOLUTION IS TO EXPLORE NEW PLACES IN THE MEADOW AND MEET NEW FRIENDS ALONG THE WAY.

DID YOU KNOW?

SHARING SPECIAL FOODS IS A COMMON WAY TO CELEBRATE NEW YEAR'S AROUND THE WORLD. FOR EXAMPLE, IN JAPAN, EATING LONG NOODLES SYMBOLIZES A LONG LIFE AHEAD. RABBITS ARE KNOWN FOR THEIR LOVE OF VEGETABLES, ESPECIALLY CARROTS, ALTHOUGH IN THE WILD, THEY ACTUALLY EAT A VARIETY OF GREENS. BY SHARING FOOD, RABBIT SHOWS KINDNESS AND THE JOY OF GIVING—AN IMPORTANT LESSON FOR THE NEW YEAR!

ON NEW YEAR'S DAY

REMY THE RACCOON SCURRIED AROUND THE SNOWY FOREST CLEARING, HIS SEQUINED VEST SPARKLING UNDER THE WINTER SUN. IN EACH PAW, HE HELD A CONFETTI POPPER, READY TO ADD A BURST OF COLOR TO THE NEW YEAR'S CELEBRATION. KNOWN FOR HIS PLAYFUL NATURE, REMY WAS THE ONE TO COUNT ON FOR EXTRA EXCITEMENT! AS THE COUNTDOWN TO NOON APPROACHED, HE PRACTICED POPPING CONFETTI, EACH ONE FILLING THE AIR WITH BITS OF COLORFUL PAPER. WHEN THE BIG MOMENT ARRIVED, REMY JUMPED IN DELIGHT, FILLING THE FOREST WITH CHEER AND LAUGHTER, MAKING THE NEW YEAR'S CELEBRATION EVEN MORE MEMORABLE.

REMY THE RACCOON

KINDNESS GOAL:
REMY'S *KINDNESS GOAL IS TO HELP CLEAN UP AFTER EACH CELEBRATION, ENSURING THE FOREST STAYS TIDY AND BEAUTIFUL FOR EVERYONE.*

RESOLUTION:
REMY'S RESOLUTION IS TO FIND NEW WAYS TO SURPRISE HIS FRIENDS WITH FUN GAMES AND SILLY TRICKS.

DID YOU KNOW?

IN MANY PLACES, PEOPLE CELEBRATE THE NEW YEAR BY TOSSING CONFETTI OR STREAMERS FOR GOOD LUCK. RACCOONS ARE CURIOUS ANIMALS, OFTEN ATTRACTED TO SHINY OR INTERESTING OBJECTS, AND HAVE DEXTEROUS PAWS THAT ALLOW THEM TO HOLD AND EXAMINE ITEMS. LIKE REMY, REAL RACCOONS ARE KNOWN FOR THEIR PLAYFUL AND CURIOUS NATURE, EXPLORING EVERYTHING AROUND THEM!

ON NEW YEAR'S DAY

DAISY THE DEER MOVED GRACEFULLY THROUGH THE FOREST, HER ANTLERS ADORNED WITH A GARLAND OF WINTER LEAVES AND FLOWERS. SHE CAREFULLY PLACED BERRIES AND PINECONES ON THE BRANCHES OF A TREE, CREATING A BEAUTIFUL, NATURAL DECORATION FOR THE NEW YEAR'S CELEBRATION. DAISY LOVED ADDING GENTLE TOUCHES OF BEAUTY TO HER SURROUNDINGS, MAKING THE FOREST FEEL WARM AND WELCOMING FOR HER FRIENDS. AS THE OTHER ANIMALS ARRIVED, THEY ADMIRED DAISY'S PEACEFUL DECORATIONS, FEELING CALM AND JOYFUL AS THEY GATHERED TO CELEBRATE TOGETHER.

DAISY THE DEER

KINDNESS GOAL:
DAISY'S KINDNESS GOAL IS TO HELP OTHER ANIMALS FIND FOOD IN THE FOREST WHEN THE WEATHER IS HARSH, ENSURING EVERYONE STAYS HEALTHY.

RESOLUTION:
DAISY'S RESOLUTION IS TO EXPLORE NEW PARTS OF THE FOREST AND FIND DIFFERENT FLOWERS AND PLANTS TO SHARE WITH HER FRIENDS.

DID YOU KNOW?

MANY PEOPLE AROUND THE WORLD DECORATE THEIR HOMES FOR THE NEW YEAR, OFTEN WITH FLOWERS OR GREENERY TO SYMBOLIZE GROWTH AND RENEWAL. DEER, TOO, PLAY AN IMPORTANT ROLE IN NATURE BY SPREADING SEEDS AND HELPING FORESTS GROW AS THEY MOVE THROUGH DIFFERENT AREAS. THEIR PRESENCE HELPS KEEP THE FOREST HEALTHY AND THRIVING!

ON NEW YEAR'S DAY

DOTTIE THE DUCKLING WADDLED THROUGH THE FOREST, EACH STEP CAUSING HER LITTLE PARTY CROWN TO TILT SLIGHTLY. SHE WAS THE SMALLEST IN THE GROUP, BUT HER EXCITEMENT WAS AS BIG AS ANYONE'S. IN HER PERFECT LITTLE LINE, SHE LED HER DUCKLING SIBLINGS TO THE NEW YEAR'S GATHERING, QUACKING HAPPILY AS THEY MARCHED THROUGH THE SNOW. EACH WORE A COLORFUL CROWN, BRINGING BRIGHT POPS OF COLOR TO THE SNOWY FOREST. WHEN THEY REACHED THE CELEBRATION, DOTTIE GAVE A PROUD LITTLE QUACK, THRILLED TO BE PART OF THE FESTIVITIES AND READY TO CHEER IN THE NEW YEAR.

DOTTIE THE DUCKLING

KINDNESS GOAL:
DOTTIE'S KINDNESS GOAL IS TO HELP HER SIBLINGS FIND FOOD AND SHARE TREATS DURING THEIR ADVENTURES.

RESOLUTION:
DOTTIE'S RESOLUTION IS TO BE BRAVE AND TRY SWIMMING IN A NEW PART OF THE POND THIS SPRING.

DID YOU KNOW?

PARADES ARE A COMMON WAY TO CELEBRATE NEW YEAR'S AROUND THE WORLD, FULL OF COLORFUL COSTUMES AND HAPPY CROWDS. DUCKLINGS, LIKE MANY OTHER YOUNG ANIMALS, INSTINCTIVELY FOLLOW THEIR PARENT IN A LINE TO STAY SAFE AND TOGETHER. THIS BEHAVIOR IS CALLED "IMPRINTING," WHERE YOUNG ANIMALS LEARN TO STAY CLOSE AND FOLLOW A LEADER.

ON NEW YEAR'S DAY

HAZEL THE HEDGEHOG TIPTOED THROUGH THE FOREST, FEELING A LITTLE SHY BUT EXCITED FOR THE NEW YEAR'S CELEBRATION. SHE WORE A FESTIVE BOW AROUND HER NECK, AND HER QUILLS WERE SPRINKLED WITH SOFT FLOWER-PETAL CONFETTI SHE HAD GATHERED FROM THE FOREST FLOOR. HAZEL LOVED ADDING LITTLE TOUCHES OF BEAUTY, EVEN THOUGH SHE PREFERRED STAYING IN THE BACKGROUND. AS SHE REACHED THE CLEARING, HAZEL GAVE A GENTLE SHAKE, RELEASING THE PETALS INTO THE AIR. THEY FLOATED DOWN LIKE SNOWFLAKES, CATCHING THE LIGHT FROM THE LANTERNS ABOVE. HER FRIENDS LAUGHED AND CLAPPED, MARVELING AT THE COLORFUL DISPLAY. HAZEL SMILED TO HERSELF, FEELING PROUD AND HAPPY TO HAVE BROUGHT A LITTLE EXTRA MAGIC TO THE CELEBRATION. THOUGH SHE WAS QUIET, HAZEL'S SPECIAL TOUCH MADE EVERYONE FEEL A LITTLE MORE JOYFUL AS THEY WELCOMED THE NEW YEAR.

HAZEL THE HEDGEHOG

KINDNESS GOAL:
HAZEL'S KINDNESS GOAL IS TO MAKE HER FRIENDS LITTLE FLOWER-PETAL SURPRISES WHENEVER THEY FEEL DOWN, TO BRIGHTEN THEIR DAY.

RESOLUTION:
HAZEL'S RESOLUTION IS TO BE BRAVER AND JOIN IN MORE ACTIVITIES WITH HER FRIENDS.

DID YOU KNOW?

AROUND THE WORLD, CELEBRATIONS OFTEN INCLUDE SPECIAL TOUCHES THAT BRING JOY AND SURPRISE, LIKE COLORFUL LIGHTS, DECORATIONS, OR CONFETTI. HEDGEHOGS, WITH THEIR UNIQUE QUILLS, PLAY AN IMPORTANT ROLE IN NATURE BY AERATING THE SOIL AS THEY DIG AND FORAGE, HELPING PLANTS GROW. THOUGH THEY ARE NATURALLY SHY, HEDGEHOGS REMIND US THAT EVEN SMALL, QUIET CONTRIBUTIONS CAN MAKE A BIG DIFFERENCE IN THE WORLD AROUND US.

ON NEW YEAR'S DAY

MILLIE THE MOUSE SCURRIED AROUND THE SNOWY FOREST, WEARING A SPARKLY HEADBAND WITH LITTLE STARS AND A TINY NOISEMAKER HANGING AROUND HER NECK. THOUGH SHE WAS SMALL, MILLIE WAS FULL OF EXCITEMENT AS SHE SET UP HER DECORATIONS. CAREFULLY, SHE ARRANGED TINY PINECONES AND BERRIES IN A NEAT PATTERN ON THE GROUND, CREATING A FESTIVE TOUCH FOR THE NEW YEAR'S CELEBRATION. MILLIE LOVED HELPING, AND HER FRIENDS ALWAYS APPRECIATED HER CAREFUL ATTENTION TO DETAIL. AS THE OTHER ANIMALS ARRIVED, THEY MARVELED AT HER WORK AND CHEERED HER ON, MAKING MILLIE'S HEART SWELL WITH PRIDE. SHE SQUEAKED HAPPILY, READY TO COUNT DOWN TO THE NEW YEAR WITH EVERYONE.

MILLIE THE MOUSE

KINDNESS GOAL:
MILLIE'S KINDNESS GOAL IS TO HELP HER FRIENDS FIND SMALL TREASURES IN THE FOREST TO BRIGHTEN THEIR DAYS.

RESOLUTION:
MILLIE'S RESOLUTION IS TO BE BRAVE AND TRY NEW ACTIVITIES, EVEN IF THEY SEEM A LITTLE BIG FOR HER.

DID YOU KNOW?

EVEN SMALL CONTRIBUTIONS CAN HAVE A BIG IMPACT, AS MANY TRADITIONS AROUND THE WORLD CELEBRATE THE NEW YEAR WITH THOUGHTFUL DECORATIONS AND PERSONAL TOUCHES. MICE ARE KNOWN FOR THEIR RESOURCEFULNESS, OFTEN CREATING COZY NESTS FROM SMALL BITS OF NATURE. MILLIE'S CREATIVITY MIRRORS THE WAY REAL MICE CAREFULLY USE WHAT'S AROUND THEM TO MAKE THEIR HOMES SPECIAL.

ON NEW YEAR'S DAY

BELLA THE BLUEBIRD PERCHED ON A HIGH BRANCH, PRACTICING HER CHEERFUL SONG FOR THE NEW YEAR'S CELEBRATION. WITH A TINY GOLDEN MICROPHONE AND A SMALL BOW ON HER WING, SHE FELT READY TO LEAD THE ANIMALS IN SONG. BELLA LOVED HOW MUSIC BROUGHT EVERYONE TOGETHER, AND HER VOICE FILLED THE SNOWY FOREST WITH WARMTH AND HAPPINESS. AS HER FRIENDS GATHERED BELOW, BELLA TOOK A DEEP BREATH AND BEGAN HER SONG. THE NOTES SOARED THROUGH THE TREES, CARRYING JOY TO EVERY CORNER OF THE FOREST. THE OTHER ANIMALS CLAPPED AND CHEERED, FEELING THE MAGIC OF THE NEW YEAR IN BELLA'S MELODY. SHE SMILED PROUDLY, KNOWING HER SONG HAD MADE THE CELEBRATION TRULY SPECIAL.

BELLA THE BLUEBIRD

KINDNESS GOAL:
BELLA'S KINDNESS GOAL IS TO VISIT FRIENDS WHO MAY FEEL LONELY AND CHEER THEM UP WITH A SONG.

RESOLUTION:
BELLA'S RESOLUTION IS TO LEARN A NEW SONG TO SHARE WITH HER FRIENDS EACH SEASON.

DID YOU KNOW?

SINGING IS A UNIVERSAL WAY TO CELEBRATE NEW YEAR'S, FROM SONGS LIKE "AULD LANG SYNE" TO FESTIVE CAROLS IN MANY LANGUAGES. BLUEBIRDS, LIKE BELLA, ARE NATURAL SINGERS, USING THEIR UNIQUE SONGS TO COMMUNICATE WITH EACH OTHER. THEIR MELODIES BRING BEAUTY TO THE FOREST, MUCH LIKE MUSIC BRINGS PEOPLE TOGETHER IN CELEBRATIONS.

ON NEW YEAR'S DAY

FELLIE THE FROG SHIVERED SLIGHTLY AS HE HOPPED THROUGH THE SNOWY FOREST, HIS COZY SCARF WRAPPED TIGHTLY AROUND HIM. NORMALLY, FELLIE PREFERRED WARM PONDS AND SUNNY DAYS, BUT HE DIDN'T WANT TO MISS THE NEW YEAR'S CELEBRATION WITH HIS FRIENDS. CAREFULLY, HE LEAPT FROM ONE DRY SPOT TO ANOTHER, AVOIDING THE SNOW AS MUCH AS POSSIBLE. WHEN HE REACHED THE CLEARING, HE WARMED UP BY HOPPING IN HAPPY CIRCLES, SHOWING OFF HIS SILLY DANCE MOVES. THE OTHER ANIMALS CHEERED AND LAUGHED, DELIGHTED BY FELLIE'S ANTICS. DESPITE THE CHILL, FELLIE'S JOY FOR THE NEW YEAR MADE EVERYONE FEEL WARMER.

FELLIE THE FROG

KINDNESS GOAL:
FELLIE'S KINDNESS GOAL IS TO TEACH HIS FRIENDS FUN HOPPING GAMES AND DANCES TO MAKE THEM SMILE ALL YEAR ROUND.

RESOLUTION:
FELLIE'S RESOLUTION IS TO FIND MORE SUNNY ROCKS BY THE POND FOR EXTRA RELAXATION TIME DURING WARM DAYS..

DID YOU KNOW?

FROGS ARE SENSITIVE TO COLD BECAUSE THEY ARE AMPHIBIANS AND RELY ON THEIR ENVIRONMENT TO REGULATE THEIR BODY TEMPERATURE. IN WINTER, SOME FROGS HIBERNATE BY BURROWING INTO MUD OR HIDING IN COZY SPOTS. EVEN IN COLDER WEATHER, FELLIE'S SPIRIT REMINDS US THAT A LITTLE BRAVERY AND JOY CAN WARM UP ANY OCCASION!

ON NEW YEAR'S DAY

FREDDIE THE FIREFLY HOVERED NEAR THE EDGE OF THE FOREST, ADJUSTING HIS TINY TOP HAT AND CHECKING THE GLOW OF HIS TAIL. HE AND THE OTHER FIREFLIES WERE READY TO LIGHT UP THE SNOWY CLEARING FOR THE NEW YEAR'S CELEBRATION. "IT'S ALMOST TIME!" FREDDIE BUZZED EXCITEDLY, LEADING THE GROUP INTO THE CLEARING. AS THE COUNTDOWN ENDED, FREDDIE AND HIS FRIENDS DANCED IN THE AIR, CREATING A MAGICAL LIGHT SHOW THAT SPARKLED LIKE STARS. THE OTHER ANIMALS CLAPPED AND CHEERED, AMAZED BY THE BEAUTIFUL DISPLAY. FREDDIE GLOWED EVEN BRIGHTER, PROUD TO HAVE BROUGHT SO MUCH JOY TO THE CELEBRATION.

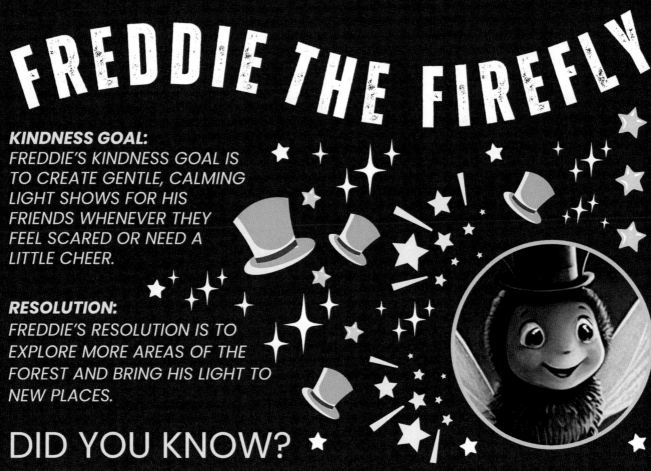

FREDDIE THE FIREFLY

KINDNESS GOAL:
FREDDIE'S KINDNESS GOAL IS TO CREATE GENTLE, CALMING LIGHT SHOWS FOR HIS FRIENDS WHENEVER THEY FEEL SCARED OR NEED A LITTLE CHEER.

RESOLUTION:
FREDDIE'S RESOLUTION IS TO EXPLORE MORE AREAS OF THE FOREST AND BRING HIS LIGHT TO NEW PLACES.

DID YOU KNOW?

AROUND THE WORLD, FIREWORKS LIGHT UP THE SKY TO CELEBRATE NEW YEAR'S, SYMBOLIZING JOY AND EXCITEMENT FOR THE YEAR AHEAD. FIREFLIES, LIKE FREDDIE, CREATE THEIR OWN "FIREWORKS" BY LIGHTING UP THEIR TAILS THROUGH A NATURAL PROCESS CALLED BIOLUMINESCENCE. THEY USE THIS GLOW TO COMMUNICATE AND ATTRACT MATES, ADDING MAGIC TO WARM SUMMER NIGHTS.

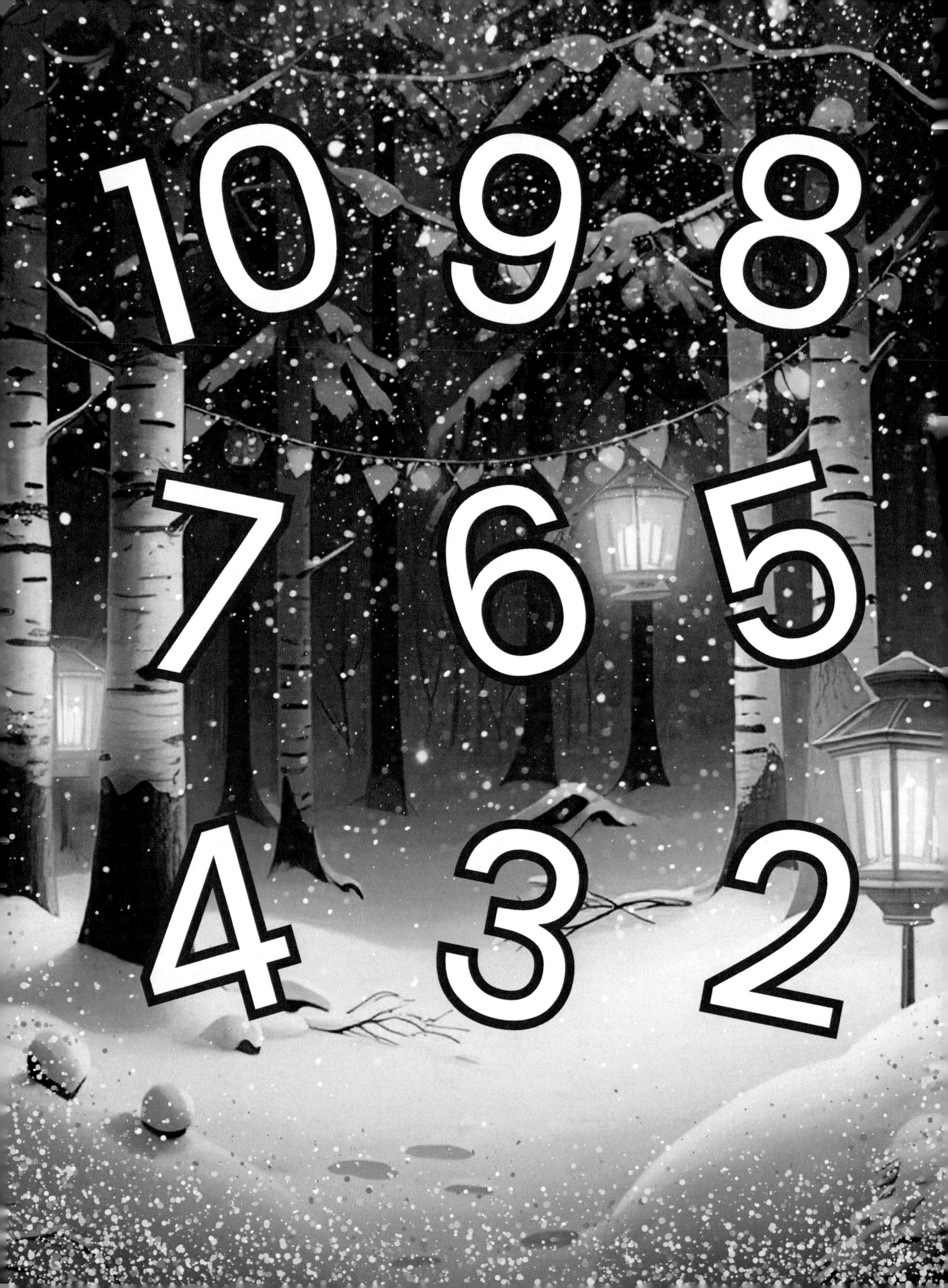
10 9 8
7 6 5
4 3 2

ON NEW YEAR'S DAY

AS THE JOYFUL CHEERS OF THE NEW YEAR'S CELEBRATION BEGAN TO FADE, BRODY THE BEAR STOOD AT THE EDGE OF THE SNOWY CLEARING, TAKING A FINAL LOOK AT THE MAGICAL SCENE BEHIND HIM. THE SOFT GLOW OF LANTERNS STILL ILLUMINATED THE FOREST, THEIR LIGHT REFLECTING OFF THE SNOW LIKE A BLANKET OF TINY STARS. CONFETTI SPARKLED ON THE GROUND, A REMINDER OF THE HAPPY CELEBRATION SHARED WITH HIS FRIENDS. THE TREE BRANCHES, STILL ADORNED WITH PINECONES AND BERRIES, GENTLY SWAYED IN THE WINTER BREEZE, AS IF WAVING GOODBYE TO THE DAY.

BRODY ADJUSTED HIS COZY SCARF, THE ONE WITH THE LITTLE STARS, AND GAVE A CONTENTED SIGH. HIS HEART FELT WARM DESPITE THE CHILLY AIR. HE GLANCED BACK AT THE CLEARING WHERE THE LAUGHTER OF HIS FRIENDS LINGERED, FILLING THE FOREST WITH A LINGERING SENSE OF JOY. HE SAW DAISY THE DEER CAREFULLY GATHERING PINECONES, FERGUS THE FOX TWIRLING HIS SHINY RIBBON, AND HAZEL THE HEDGEHOG SOFTLY SHAKING OFF THE LAST BITS OF PETAL CONFETTI FROM HER QUILLS.

WITH A WIDE, PROUD GRIN, BRODY WAVED ONE LAST TIME, KNOWING HE HAD HELPED MAKE THIS MOMENT SPECIAL. HOSTING THE GATHERING IN HIS COZY DEN, ENSURING EVERYONE FELT WELCOME AND CARED FOR, WAS HIS FAVORITE WAY TO START THE YEAR. AS HE TURNED TO HEAD BACK INTO THE FOREST, HE FELT A SPARK OF EXCITEMENT FOR THE DAYS AHEAD—NEW MEMORIES, MORE CELEBRATIONS, AND COUNTLESS ADVENTURES WITH THE FRIENDS HE CHERISHED MOST.

THE SNOW CRUNCHED SOFTLY UNDER HIS PAWS AS BRODY MADE HIS WAY HOME, HIS HEART FULL AND HIS MIND REPLAYING THE HAPPY MOMENTS OF THE DAY. HE GLANCED OVER HIS SHOULDER ONE LAST TIME, HIS JOYFUL GAZE CAPTURING THE MAGICAL GLOW OF THE CLEARING. WITH A QUIET CHUCKLE, HE WHISPERED TO HIMSELF, "WHAT A PERFECT WAY TO WELCOME THE NEW YEAR."

Brody smiled and thought, I wonder what adventures this new year will bring?

ON NEW YEAR'S DAY

AS THE CELEBRATION BEGAN TO WIND DOWN, REMY THE RACCOON GRABBED HIS LITTLE BROOM AND GOT STRAIGHT TO WORK. THE SNOWY CLEARING SPARKLED WITH COLORFUL CONFETTI, AND REMY WANTED TO MAKE SURE THE FOREST STAYED AS BEAUTIFUL AS IT HAD BEEN FOR THE NEW YEAR'S FESTIVITIES. WITH A CHEERFUL HUM, HE SWEPT UP THE BITS OF PAPER INTO A NEAT PILE, PAUSING EVERY NOW AND THEN TO ADMIRE HOW THE LANTERNS STILL CAST A WARM GLOW OVER THE SCENE.

"THIS HAS BEEN SUCH A SPECIAL DAY," REMY SAID ALOUD, HIS VOICE CARRYING A HINT OF PRIDE. "BUT KEEPING MY RESOLUTIONS STARTS NOW!" HE STRAIGHTENED HIS SEQUINED VEST AND SWEPT FASTER, THINKING OF HOW NICE IT WOULD BE FOR HIS FRIENDS TO WAKE UP TO A TIDY FOREST.

AS THE CLEARING GREW CLEANER, REMY THOUGHT ABOUT THE YEAR AHEAD. THERE WOULD BE MORE PARTIES, MORE LAUGHTER, AND CERTAINLY MORE CHANCES TO ADD HIS PLAYFUL TOUCH TO EVERY GATHERING. BUT THIS YEAR, HE ALSO WANTED TO SHOW THAT EVEN SMALL EFFORTS—LIKE CLEANING UP AFTER THE FUN—COULD MAKE A BIG DIFFERENCE.

WHEN THE LAST BIT OF CONFETTI WAS SCOOPED UP, REMY STOOD BACK AND ADMIRED HIS WORK. THE FOREST WAS PEACEFUL NOW, THE SNOW SPARKLING UNDER THE SOFT LIGHT OF THE MOON. HE SMILED, HIS HEART WARM WITH THE THOUGHT OF THE WONDERFUL MEMORIES THEY'D CREATED THAT DAY.

WITH ONE FINAL GLANCE AT THE CLEARING, REMY WHISPERED, "HERE'S TO A BRIGHT NEW YEAR—AND A FOREST FULL OF FUN, KINDNESS, AND A LITTLE SPARKLE!"

ADJUSTING HIS VEST, REMY PADDED OFF INTO THE TREES, EXCITED FOR ALL THE ADVENTURES THE YEAR WOULD BRING.

A little cleanup today makes the forest sparkle for tomorrow!

ON NEW YEAR'S DAY

AS THE FESTIVITIES CAME TO AN END, MILLIE THE MOUSE SCAMPERED TOWARD HER COZY BURROW, THE SNOWY FOREST GLOWING SOFTLY UNDER THE LIGHT OF THE LANTERNS AND A SHIMMERING MOON. HER SPARKLY HEADBAND WOBBLED GENTLY WITH EACH HOP, AND THE TINY NOISEMAKER AROUND HER NECK JINGLED FAINTLY, REMINDING HER OF THE JOYFUL CELEBRATION SHE HAD JUST SHARED WITH HER FRIENDS.

MILLIE'S HEART WAS WARM WITH HAPPINESS AS SHE THOUGHT ABOUT ALL THE FUN THEY'D HAD. SHE SMILED AS SHE REMEMBERED FERGUS THE FOX LEADING THE PARADE, DAISY THE DEER'S BEAUTIFUL DECORATIONS, AND BRODY THE BEAR'S COZY SEATING ARRANGEMENTS. SHE FELT PROUD OF HER OWN LITTLE CONTRIBUTIONS TOO—THE TINY PINECONE AND BERRY PATTERNS SHE'D ARRANGED HAD BROUGHT CHEERFUL SMILES TO EVERYONE.

AS MILLIE REACHED HER BURROW, SHE PAUSED AT THE ENTRANCE TO GLANCE BACK AT THE CLEARING, WHERE A FEW LANTERNS STILL FLICKERED IN THE DISTANCE. WHAT A WONDERFUL START TO THE YEAR! SHE THOUGHT. HER MIND BEGAN TO WANDER AS SHE PLANNED HOW TO FULFILL HER RESOLUTIONS. "THIS YEAR, I'LL BE BRAVER," SHE WHISPERED TO HERSELF. "I'LL EXPLORE THE PARTS OF THE FOREST I'VE ALWAYS BEEN TOO NERVOUS TO VISIT. WHO KNOWS WHAT TREASURES I'LL FIND?"

SHE SCURRIED INSIDE, THE WARMTH OF HER BURROW EMBRACING HER LIKE AN OLD FRIEND. SETTLING DOWN WITH A SOFT TUFT OF MOSS, SHE THOUGHT OF HER KINDNESS GOAL. "AND MAYBE I'LL BRING BACK SOME OF THOSE TREASURES FOR MY FRIENDS," SHE MUSED, HER WHISKERS TWITCHING WITH EXCITEMENT. "A LITTLE GIFT CAN BRIGHTEN ANYONE'S DAY."

MILLIE SNUGGLED INTO HER NEST, HER THOUGHTS DANCING WITH IDEAS FOR ADVENTURES, TREASURES, AND WAYS TO MAKE HER FRIENDS SMILE. AS SHE CLOSED HER EYES, THE GLOW OF THE CELEBRATION AND THE PROMISE OF THE NEW YEAR FILLED HER HEART WITH HOPE. TOMORROW IS A NEW DAY, SHE THOUGHT. I CAN'T WAIT TO SEE WHERE IT LEADS.

Even the smallest steps can lead to the biggest adventures!

OTHER TITLES YOU MAY ENJOY

ON MONSTER MOUNTAIN

ON CAMPFIRE NIGHT

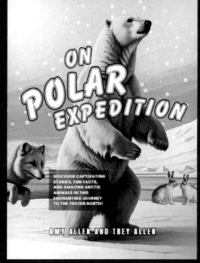

ON POLAR EXPEDITION

ON CHRISTMAS BALLET

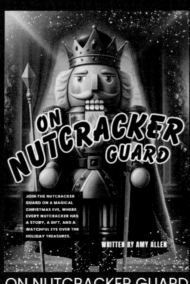

ON NUTCRACKER GUARD

ON CHRISTMAS EVE

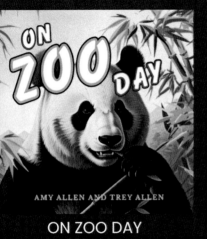

ON ZOO DAY

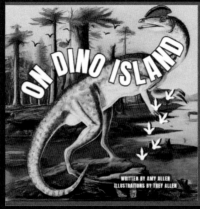

ON DINO ISLAND

ON OCEAN QUEST

AVAILABLE ON AMAZON

Made in the USA
Coppell, TX
29 December 2024

43645372R10024